Grandpa Lou folded his arms. "You must have taken my book with you downstairs."

"I don't think so, Pop," said Stu. "But we'll take a look, okay?"

Grandpa Lou grumbled as they started down the stairs. "It will take hours to look through that messy workshop of yours. And if we don't find it, I'll be sure to tell the library police it was YOU who lost it!"

Rugrats Chapter Books

Book 'Em, TOMMY!

KLASKY
CSUPO INC.

Based on the TV series *Rugrats*® created by Arlene Klasky, Gabor Csupo,
and Paul Germain as seen on Nickelodeon®

SIMON SPOTLIGHT

An imprint of Simon & Schuster Children's Publishing Division
1230 Avenue of the Americas, New York, New York 10020

Manufactured in the United States of America

First Edition

2 4 6 8 10 9 7 5 3 1

ISBN 0-689-83124-2

Library of Congress Catalog Card Number 99-76382

Book 'Em, TOMMY!

by Maria Rosado
illustrated by Gary Fields

Simon Spotlight/Nickelodeon

New York   London   Toronto   Sydney   Singapore

Chapter 1

"Look, Tommy, that tree is talking!" Chuckie said as he grabbed Tommy's arm. He pointed at the TV.

Tommy and Chuckie had been playing with Phil, Lil, and Angelica in the playpen all morning. Tommy's dad, Stu, and his grandpa, Lou, were watching TV.

"I've never seen a tree talk, Chuckie," Tommy said. But sure enough, a tree was talking on TV. The tree waved two big branches in the air as it shouted, "Come to Monty's Tree House for all your garden supplies right now! It's our annual blooming sale!"

"Sale?" asked Didi as she poked her head into the living room. "Did I hear someone say sale?"

"Wasn't me," said Stu.

"Or me," said Grandpa Lou.

On TV, the tree was still talking. "And don't forget! This may be your last chance to buy bulbs! So hurry on over."

"Stu! Did you hear that? This may be our last chance!" Didi said. She looked out the window. "But the yard isn't ready yet. I haven't even begun to dig a garden."

"Maybe our buddy Spike can help," Stu suggested. "He's been digging up holes all week."

Didi shook her head. "But then Spike

fills them up again. It would take us days to dig up enough of his old holes." She sighed. "But I really would like to plant some bulbs!"

In the playpen Chuckie looked over at Tommy. "Why does your mommy want to plant bulbs, Tommy?"

"I dunno, Chuckie." Tommy wrinkled his brow and shook his head. It sounded funny to him, too.

Angelica rolled her eyes. "You babies are soooo dumb. Don't you know flowers need light to grow? That's why they plant lightbulbs!"

Just then they heard Stu say, "You go get the flower bulbs, Deed. Pop and I will watch the kids."

Didi thought for a minute. Last week Stu was so busy working on a new invention that he forgot about the babies. And somehow Dil's banana baby food had found its way into the VCR. Didi was still cleaning the sticky stuff out of the machine. She wondered if she should stay home. "Uh, Stu," Didi began to say.

But Angelica had another idea. "Don't worry, Aunt Didi! I'll help watch the babies!" Angelica said in her sweetest voice. It was much more fun when Stu and Grandpa Lou were baby-sitting. Angelica usually got her way with the babies then. And today she had plans for a jar of mushed peas. She blinked her big eyes. "We'll be just fine!"

"Um, thanks, Angelica," said Didi absently as she took another look at the backyard. It did seem very empty.

"Tigerflowers! I have to get tigerflowers," Didi muttered. "And lilies! I need to plant lots of lilies. Oh, I'll never have time to dig holes for them all!"

Didi grabbed her purse and turned to Stu and Grandpa Lou. "Okay, I'm going to get the bulbs," she said. "I'll take Dil with me. Now, be sure to watch the babies, Stu. And keep an eye on that banana baby food."

Stu looked at Grandpa Lou. "Don't I always?" he asked. Grandpa Lou nodded. "Don't worry, Deed, the Pickles men have got it covered."

When Didi left, Lil said to Tommy, "Your mommy said she was planting Lils out there. How will you guys know it's me if there are lots of Lils? I have to be the only Lil."

"Right," said Phil. "One Lil is plenty!"

"What do you mean, Philip?" asked Lil.

"I mean no more Lils, Lillian!" said Phil. "If there are more Lils, there have to be more Phils!"

Tommy tried to imagine a backyard

full of Phils and Lils. How would they ever find the real Lil and Phil?

Chuckie was worried too. "Your mommy said tigerflowers! Are they going to chase us? Are they going to bite us? What'll we do?"

Angelica sighed. "Oh, babies," she said. "Tigerflowers are plants. So are lilies. Aunt Didi wants to dig up the backyard to plant flowers."

Suddenly Grandpa Lou leaped off the couch. "Wait a minute! All this talk about digging reminds me. I *have* to return that library book."

"Which book, Pop?" Stu asked.

"It's called *Old Bones*," Grandpa Lou said. "I thought it was about old folks like me. Turns out it's about digging up dinosaur bones! Now where did I leave that book?"

"I'll help you look, Pop," Stu said,

getting up from the couch. "But I'm sure the library won't mind if it's a little overdue."

"That's what you think," said Grandpa Lou. "If I don't return that book today, it'll be overdue, and then they'll sniff *me* out. And I'll have to pay, for sure!"

"What does Grandpa Lou mean, Angelica?" Tommy asked when the grown-ups had left.

Angelica thought hard. "Well, when grown-ups have a lie-berry book too long, it gets over-goo," she said. "That means it gets covered in yucky, smelly goo."

Tommy and Chuckie wrinkled their noses. Phil and Lil licked their lips.

"Mmmm," said Lil. "Yummy!"

Angelica leaned closer toward the babies. "And when it starts to smell really bad," she said with a mischievous grin, "they send out the Sniffer."

"The Sniffer?" Chuckie asked. He did not like the sound of that.

"The Sniffer can smell stinky lie-berry books," said Angelica. "It has a giant nose that can smell just about anything. And real big teeth."

"Big teeth?" wondered Chuckie nervously.

"The Sniffer sniffs up lie-berry books and anything or anybody around them! Right up his big, giant nose! Just like that!"

The babies gulped.

"Stop it, Angelica!" Chuckie cried. "Is that true?"

Angelica laughed just as the babies heard a sound in the hallway. *Thump-thump. Thump-thump-thump.*

Suddenly Angelica got really quiet.

"Who's that?" asked Phil, grabbing Lil's arm.

Then they all heard another noise. It was louder. *Sniff-sniff. Sniff-sniff-sniff.*

"What's that?" asked Lil, grabbing Phil's arm.

"I know what it is," Chuckie said. He was shaking. "It's the Sniffer!"

Chapter 2

The thumping sound came again. The sniffing got louder. Suddenly a huge creature rushed through the door and ran toward the playpen.

Chuckie covered his face. "Help me, Tommy!" he yelled.

"It's okay, Chuckie," Tommy said. "It's only Spike!"

Chuckie slowly took his hands away from his eyes.

Sniff-sniff. Spike could smell a cherry lollipop in Chuckie's pocket. *Thump-thump* went Spike's tail against the wall.

Chuckie laughed with relief. "That lie-berry book must smell like a lollipop!"

"I knew it was Spike the whole time," sniffed Angelica.

Just then Grandpa Lou came back, holding a book in his hand. "I found it!"

Hearing Grandpa Lou, Stu rushed in and took a look. The book was filled with pictures of dinosaurs and their bones. He flipped the pages of the book. "That's it!" Stu shouted.

"Didn't I say so?" asked Grandpa Lou.

"No, Pop. I mean, that's the idea I need to fix my last invention." Stu pointed to a picture of some people digging with little spades. "They could have done a lot more if they'd had the Pickles Snow Shovel 3000 Deluxe."

Stu had built the Pickles Snow Shovel 3000 Deluxe to shovel snow. It was a funny-looking contraption. There was a big plastic yellow spade at the end for shoveling, and at the top was a wheel from a baby carriage.

The invention worked fine, at first. But the problem began when the machine would not stop digging. When Stu was finally able to stop the snow shovel, it had dug a hole so deep that Didi was sure they were going to find oil. But they never did. They just had a really deep hole until Stu filled it back up.

"My machine can dig up dinosaur bones instead of shoveling snow," Stu said now as he headed downstairs. "If I can just turn that gear to the left . . . hey, Pop, want to give me a hand?"

Grandpa Lou sighed. "Okay," he said as he followed his son to the basement.

When the men had gone downstairs, Tommy took out his screwdriver. He opened the gate of the playpen with one quick turn. He wanted to look at that book. So did Chuckie, Phil, and Lil.

Tommy slid the book off the table and opened it. The other babies gathered around.

"Oooh," said Lil, pointing at a picture. "Lookit all those holes! Your mom could plant a lot of bulbs there, Tommy."

Then Tommy dropped the book on the floor, and it opened to a picture of a dinosaur. Chuckie took a quick look—that dinosaur reminded him of Reptar.

"I wanna see," Angelica said, trying to look over Chuckie's shoulder. But Phil and Lil took the book and disappeared into the kitchen.

"Hey!" Angelica yelled. "Come back!"

But Phil and Lil didn't hear her. After

a few minutes they came back with the book, and Angelica grabbed it away. "Babies shouldn't touch lie-berry books! You can't even read!"

"Can you, Angelica?" Tommy asked.

"Of course!" Angelica sat on the floor and began to open the book—only it was upside down. She turned a page. "This is soooo interesting!"

They watched Angelica turn another page. Phil yawned.

"Let's play hide-and-go-peek," said Lil. The babies toddled off. Chuckie was It. He looked behind the couch for the other babies. He looked under the chair. Then he looked behind the couch again.

Angelica stared at Chuckie. She left the book on the table and stood up.

"You babies can't do anything right!" Angelica pointed to the feet that were peeking out from under the curtains.

"There they are! Now I'm going to be It!"

"Okay, Angelica," said Tommy. He went to take another look at the book before finding a hiding place.

"One . . . two . . . five-ten-seven!" Angelica counted. She opened one eye and called out, "Ready or not, babies, here I come!"

But before Angelica could find anyone, they heard Stu and Grandpa Lou coming up the stairs. Angelica and the babies quickly scooted back into the playpen.

"Thanks, Pop. I think we've got it," Stu said as he held up the strange-looking snow shovel.

"That's nice," replied Grandpa Lou. "Now can I return that book?"

Stu shrugged. "Sure. I don't need it anymore."

Grandpa Lou reached for the library book, but it was gone!

Chapter 3

"Now, where did that book go?" Grandpa Lou wondered as he scratched his head. "I thought I put it right there."

He looked at Stu. "I didn't take it!" Stu said.

Stu propped the snow shovel against the wall. Then he and Grandpa Lou checked all over the room. They looked under the couch, behind the couch, on the shelves, and even behind the curtains.

Grandpa Lou folded his arms. "You must have taken my book with you downstairs."

"I don't think so, Pop," said Stu. "But we'll take a look, okay?"

Grandpa Lou grumbled as they started down the stairs. "It will take hours to look through that messy workshop of yours. And if we don't find it, I'll be sure to tell the library police it was YOU who lost it!"

Stu called out to the babies, "You kids stay right there, okay? We'll be right back!"

"The lie-berry police!" Tommy said. "Did you hear that? The lie-berry police will come for my daddy if they don't find that book!"

"You mean he'll have to go to jail?" Chuckie asked.

"My daddy says the police take bad

people to a jail called Sing Sing," Angelica said.

The police! Sing Sing!

Tommy closed his eyes. He imagined what would happen if the police took his daddy to the place called Sing Sing.

At Sing Sing everyone had to sing. They dressed up in silly costumes and danced and sang onstage all day long.

Stu was miserable. He couldn't sing. He couldn't remember the words to any song. He couldn't dance. He couldn't stand it. All he wanted to do was go home to Didi and baby Dil and Tommy.

"Nooooo!" Tommy yelled. "My daddy can't go to Sing Sing!"

Chapter 4

"Tommy, are you okay?" Chuckie poked Tommy in the arm.

Tommy opened his eyes. It was just a daydream! But maybe it could happen—unless they found that book. "We gots to find the book, you guys," he said.

"Why should I help?" Angelica asked.

"You have to, Angelica," Tommy begged. "You're the oldest."

"Well . . . you got that right," Angelica

said. "Okay, but you babies have to listen to every word I say. And do everything I tell you to do."

"Okay," said Tommy.

Phil and Lil nodded their heads.

Chuckie was worried. "Are you sure that's a good idea?" he asked.

Angelica narrowed her eyes at Chuckie, then said, "What we have here is a misery. That's what you call it when you don't know something. And that means we need a detector."

"Huh?" said Tommy.

"And the bestest detector of them all is . . . Shirlylock Holmes!" said Angelica.

"First I need a magnetizing glass," she continued. "Hmm . . . I can use Chuckie's lollipop. Hand it over, Finster."

Chuckie sighed as he gave up his cherry-flavored lollipop.

"There! Now I'm ready to start

detectoring." Angelica looked through the lollipop around the room. "Aha! There's a clue!"

The babies rushed over.

"That's just Spike's squeaky toy," said Tommy.

Angelica sniffed. "I knew that!"

She looked around for some more clues, but the only thing they found was a lump of dried banana baby food.

"This is a harder case than I thought," Angelica said. "There's only one thing left to do!"

"What?" the babies all asked together.

"I have to ask you a lot of questions!"

Angelica made the babies sit in a row. Then she walked back and forth in front of them. Every once in a while she would stop and squint at them. It made the babies wiggle in their seats. After a while, Spike ran in and started following

Angelica back and forth. That made the babies giggle.

"Stop that!" Angelica barked. The babies fell silent.

"Now then, Tommy," she said softly. "I remember you were in a hurry to look at that book!"

The babies all turned to look at Tommy.

Tommy shook his head. "I just looked at it for a minute. I didn't take it."

Tommy said he had been looking at the picture of people digging in the dirt. "I was thinking that maybe our backyard would look like that when my mommy plants the lightbulbs," he said. "Then I put the book back."

"Huh," said Angelica. She turned to Chuckie. "That's when you took the book!"

Chapter 5

Chuckie sank deep into the couch. "I saw a dino-sewer who looked just like Reptar. Then I put the book back . . . I promise!" he gulped.

"Hmm," said Angelica. She thought for a minute.

"Then it's you two!" she yelled as she pointed at Phil and Lil. "You two were next! You're the one!"

"But we're two," said Lil, looking

puzzled. Phil shrugged his shoulders.

Angelica frowned. "You know what I mean."

"We only looked for a minute," said Phil.

"I liked the birdies," Lil said.

"We took the book out to the kitchen," said Phil.

"But just for a minute!" Lil added.

The twins had stacked the book on top of Spike's dish. The book made it just high enough for them to reach the cookie jar on the table.

"That was a good book," Phil said, rubbing his tummy.

"And we put it back," Lil said.

The babies all sighed. It looked like they were back where they started.

Then Tommy suddenly sat up. "Wait a minute, Angelica. You had it next!"

Chuckie nodded. So did Phil and Lil.

"That's right," they said together. "It was you!"

Angelica looked worried. Then she stopped and squinted at them. "Hey! I'm the detector here and I ask the questions, 'member?"

The babies waited.

"Since I'm the detector, I'll just ask myself," Angelica said. She put on a sickly sweet voice. "Darling Angelica, did you take that book?"

"Why, no, dear Shirlylock!" Angelica answered herself. "I just used that little pocket in the front to hide the baloney from my lunch. I hate baloney."

"That's what I thought," Shirlylock told Angelica. "I knew you were innocent!"

Then Angelica turned back to Tommy. She reminded everyone that Tommy had looked at the book again—before she was It in hide-and-go-seek.

Everyone stared at Tommy. "I just showed it to Spike because it had a big bone on the cover," he said.

Now everyone stared at Spike. "Woof, woof," barked Spike.

Chapter 6

Spike stopped following Angelica. He sat down and wagged his tail. *Thump-thump.*

That's when the babies saw all the muddy pawprints on the rug. Spike's feet were dirty. It was a sure sign he had been digging.

The babies looked at each other.

"Uh-oh," said Tommy. "Spike must have buried the book!"

The babies looked outside. There were

small piles of dirt all over the yard. Spike must have dug at least a hundred-gazillion holes.

"We'll never find it," Tommy moaned. "It's buried forever!"

"Don't cry, Tommy," Chuckie said. "We'll think of something!"

"What, Chuckie?" asked Phil.

"I dunno," said Chuckie. "Maybe that thing over there?"

He pointed at Stu's snow shovel invention.

Five minutes later the babies were dragging the snow shovel into the yard.

"Where shall we start, you guys?" asked Chuckie.

"That hole looks good," said Phil, pointing to a hole by the fence.

"This one is better," Lil said, pointing to a hole by the door.

"Oh, you babies don't know anything,"

said Angelica. "This is the best one." Angelica pointed to a hole by the tree.

"Let's start over there," said Tommy. He pointed to the biggest hole in the yard. Everyone nodded their heads, so they dragged the machine to the hole and stood it up.

"Here goes," said Tommy. He pushed the big yellow button.

Rrrrrrrrrrr! Brrrrrrrrr! The snow shovel made a loud noise as it started shoveling dirt. Pretty soon the machine was scooping all over the backyard. And everywhere it scooped, it made a hole.

The babies cheered.

A bone flew out of one hole. Then more bones, an old sneaker, a couple of squeaky toys, a dirty Binky, and even one of Cynthia's outfits.

"Hey!" said Angelica. "So that's where the Belle of the Ball gown went!"

More dirt flew through the air. But no book.

A minute later something went wrong. The snow shovel was beginning to speed up around a corner of the yard. A lot more dirt flew around.

"It's going too fast!" Chuckie yelled.

"Stop!" Tommy shouted.

Spike came running into the backyard and started chasing the machine. "Woof, woof, woof," he barked. But it looked like nothing could stop the snow shovel now.

Chapter 7

Grandpa Lou and Stu heard all the noise in the backyard. "What in tarnation is going on out here?" cried Grandpa Lou. "Your fancy snow shovel is tearing up the place!"

He took off after the machine. "You must have left it on!" shouted Grandpa Lou.

"No, I didn't!" Stu shouted back as he ran after Grandpa Lou and the snow

t least, I don't think I did."

v. Hop. The snow shovel started
...g. Grandpa Lou and Stu jumped
after it. Finally Stu took a giant leap. He
grabbed his invention in a great big hug.
"Gotcha!" said Stu as they fell over in a
puff of dirt.

Grandpa Lou pushed the yellow
button. *Fssssst.* The snow shovel was
finally silent.

Grandpa Lou looked at Angelica and
the babies. "Well, I don't know how you
sprouts got out here, but it looks like
you're okay."

Then he and Stu looked around the
yard. And both of them thought the
same thing: Didi must never see this.

Just then a voice called out, "Yoo-hoo!
Anybody home?"

It was Didi! She stepped out onto the
porch. She was carrying a large paper bag

and a small, shiny spade. "I got the bulbs," Didi said, "and I'm ready to dig—"

She stopped when she saw the yard. Her eyes opened wide. Her jaw dropped. Didi's eyes began to fill with tears.

Everyone stared at Didi. And Stu gulped.

Chapter 8

"Why, you sweet things!" Didi cried. She rushed over to give Stu a hug. Tears of joy rolled down her cheeks. "How did you do it? How did you manage to dig a garden so fast?"

"Why . . . uh . . . that is," Stu stammered.

Grandpa Lou poked him in the ribs. "We all helped!" He winked at the babies. "Didn't we, sprouts?"

Angelica smiled sweetly. "Yes, we did," she said.

But Tommy was still worried. "Sing Sing," he said softly.

Just then Didi tossed her new spade into the yard. "I guess I won't be needing this anymore," she said happily.

The spade landed on a small pile of dirt.

"Look, Tommy," said Chuckie as he pointed to where the spade had fallen. "I think that's one of Spike's holes—the last one."

Chuckie was right. Angelica and the babies began to take turns digging with Didi's spade. When it was Tommy's turn, the spade hit something hard.

The babies used their hands to dig—and there was the book! Angelica fished it out of the hole. Grandpa Lou spotted his book right away.

"Hey, there it is!" he yelled. "Yup. *Old Bones!* How did that get here? Come to think of it, how did you sprouts get out here?" He scratched his head, looking puzzled.

Stu took the book and shook off some of the dirt. "Well, we'd better get this to the library before it closes," he said. "And you know what, I'll take the kids, too. It's about time they went to the library."

"Gee, thanks, son," said Grandpa Lou. "Just don't let the library police catch you!"

The babies gasped. The library police!

Stu couldn't understand why the babies didn't want to get in the car. He had to promise them a special treat to get them inside. "It's a surprise," Stu said as he buckled them into their car seats. "You'll love it. I did when I was a baby."

The babies waited for Angelica to say

she wasn't a baby. But Angelica did not say a word. In fact, she had not said a word in a while!

Angelica was scared—too scared to be bossy! This did not make the babies feel better.

Chapter 9

At the library Stu had to push the babies through the door. Once inside, though, Angelica and the babies looked around in amazement.

"Wow!" said Angelica.

"Look at all the books, Tommy," said Chuckie.

"Yeah, but don't forget the lie-berry police!" Tommy warned.

Suddenly they spotted a huge man

dressed all in black.

"He must be the lie-berry police!" whispered Chuckie.

The man stood with his back to them in front of a desk. They could hear a scary sound. *Ker-chunk! Ker-chunk!* It sounded like big, huge teeth crunching together.

The man turned. The babies gasped.

"Hi there, kids!" he said. "Having fun at the library?" Then he waved his book in the air before heading out the door.

Stu walked toward a desk where a lady with bright yellow hair was sitting. Next to her, a teenage boy smiled cheerfully. He stamped something in a stack of books. *Ker-chunk! ker-chunk!*

When the lady heard it was the kids' first time at the library, she gushed and cooed all over the babies. The boy gently tapped Angelica's hand with his stamper when she insisted. Then Angelica, Phil, and Lil wandered off to look at some children's books on a nearby table.

"We're here to return this," Stu said. "Right on time."

He plopped *Old Bones* on her desk. The sweet-faced librarian looked at it. A little piece of lollipop was stuck to the cover. There were teeth marks along the edges. She picked up one corner of the book cover. Some dirt fell out from between the pages.

"Uh, thank you," the lady said, holding her nose. There was a strong smell of baloney. She looked inside the little pocket in the book—and pulled out a piece of squashed lunch meat.

She looked up at Stu, who simply shrugged his shoulders. Then the lady looked at the card tucked inside the

pocket. "Oh, I'm sorry, you've made a mistake," said the lady. "This book *is* overdue. It should have been back yesterday."

Tommy and Chuckie looked at each other. Oh, no—this sweet lady was the library police after all!

Chapter 10

"She's gonna send my daddy to jail," Tommy whispered to Chuckie.

"Uh-oh, you caught us! It's not my book, but it looks like I'll have to pay for it," Stu said. He didn't sound scared at all!

"She's going to make him pay, Tommy!" Chuckie whispered back. "Now she'll put handmuffs on him."

Stu held out one arm, with his hand curled into a fist.

Tommy closed one eye. He couldn't bear to see the lady put handcuffs on his daddy. But he couldn't bear to look away, either.

But the lady didn't slap handcuffs on Stu. Instead Stu opened his fist and dropped two coins into the lady's hand. "There you go," he said. "Overdue fines for one day."

The lady smiled. "Thank you! That takes care of it."

Tommy could not believe it! No jail! No Sing Sing! Just two shiny coins! The library was a wonderful place.

Stu turned to leave. But before he took two steps, the lady called to him. "Oh, sir," she said.

Tommy and Chuckie looked at each other again. What now? Did the lady change her mind?

Stu walked back to the lady. She put a

book in his hands. "May I suggest a book for you to read?" she asked. Stu stared at the title on the cover: *Men Who Make a Mess and the People Who Clean Up After Them.*

Stu smiled and shook his head. "Uh, no thanks. I know just the book we're going to get."

A few minutes later he bundled everybody back into the car. Then he handed Tommy the "treat" he had promised the babies. It was a book called *When Pigs Get Big.* There were lots of pictures showing big pigs doing all kinds of jobs. There was a teacher, a chef, a firefighter—even a farmer pig.

"When I grow up to be a big pig, I'm going to be like my daddy," said Chuckie as the babies stared at the book.

"I'm going to be a lollipop," said Lil.

"Me too," said Phil. "A red one."

Angelica smirked. "You can't grow up to be a lollipop," she said. "When I'm big, I'm going to be a princess. Or a queen. Or both." She stared dreamily into space. "Yeah . . . Princess Queen Angelica."

Chuckie nudged Tommy. "What will you be when you're a big pig, Tommy?"

Tommy grinned as he hugged the library book. "I'm gonna be the lie-berry police," he said with a laugh.

About the Author

Maria Rosado has written many children's books and magazine articles, but has read even more! She has so many books in her tiny New York City apartment that there is barely enough room for her, her husband, and their two crazy cats.

When she was growing up in New Jersey, Maria once forgot to return a library book—for ten years. She finally returned it to the library, and the librarians were so surprised to get it back that they didn't charge her a fine (it would have come to $182.50). She learned that honesty is the best policy, and that you should never leave a library book under your bed if you ever want to find it again.